**Instant SCOTTY MOORE**

(LEAD GUITARIST WITH ELVIS PRESLEY)

BY RUSS SHIPTON

GW00630796

# CONTENTS

## PIECES
### (WITH EXPLANATORY NOTES)

## TRANSCRIPTIONS
### (WITH EXPLANATORY NOTES)

First Published 1990
© Copyright International Music Publications
INSTANT SCOTTY MOORE
ISBN 0 86359 696 7  Order Ref: 17118  215-2-570
Exclusive Distributors
International Music Publications
Southend Road, Woodford Green
Essex IG8 8HN England.

*Editor:* Peter Foss
*Transcriptions:* Russ Shipton
*Cover design:* Ian Barrett
*Cover Photography:* Ron Goldby
*Production:* Peter White

# INTRODUCTION

Scotty Moore is a "legend" among today's lead guitarists. His solos on the early Elvis Presley records in the 1950's and 1960's were listened to and imitated by guitarists round the world. In Britain, players like Eric Clapton, Hank Marvin (of the Shadows) and Mark Knopfler have acknowledged the influence Scotty Moore had on their playing. This book has been specially prepared to allow beginning as well as more experienced guitarists to explore the techniques Scotty Moore used to produce his concise, appropriate and exciting solos on those great Elvis Presley tracks like That's All Right Momma, Mystery Train, Heartbreak Hotel, Jailhouse Rock, Hound Dog, Blue Suede Shoes etc. etc.

The material in this book includes lead solos and fills transcribed directly from records — which you will not find in ordinary sheet music. For ease of reading, they are presented in *both* music and tablature.

To get the most out of this book, read the tablature and music explanation carefully and work slowly through the individual techniques used by Scotty Moore that are shown and analysed on pages 5 to 11. Then try the warm-up pieces before tackling the actual transcriptions.

Enjoy your playing.

R.S.

# THE SCOTTY MOORE GUITAR STYLE

Scotty Moore was (and still is) a skilled studio and live performer — both of which amounted to more or less the same thing in the 1950's. He has been a considerable, though unheralded influence on rock, blues and country guitarists in both the U.K. and America.

As a studio musician, Scotty had to cope with songs from a variety of music areas and styles — from jazz and country to boogie and rhythm and blues. He was one of the most important of those guitarists who were in the vanguard of the rock 'n' roll movement that emerged in the mid 1950's with Elvis Presley, Carl Perkins, Bill Haley, Jerry Lee Lewis and Chuck Berry, for example. As one member of a 3-piece band with Elvis and Bill Black (on acoustic bass), Scotty had to handle some of the rhythm side of things behind the vocals — Elvis did simple strumming on many of the earlier songs — as well as produce exciting and effective introductions, fills, endings and lead breaks. All these tasks he accomplished brilliantly, though Elvis as the front man and vocalist naturally received 99% of the acclaim.

## Guitars & Effects

Scotty Moore normally played a Gibson F-hole semi-acoustic guitar for his early work with Elvis Presley, though later he also used various solid-bodied guitars that had become popular by the end of the 50's. At the start of rock 'n' roll, guitar 'effects' (distortion, wah wah, chorus etc.) were unheard of. Reverb. was the only effect that was put on the guitar sound in those days.

You could play most of the solos in this book with acoustic, semi-acoustic or electric guitar — only reverb. is used and the bends are virtually all one fret or less which can be done on light gauge acoustic strings.

## Right & Left Hand Fingering

Because he had to switch from a rhythmic bass and treble chordal style to single note or "doublestop" riffs and back again, Scotty Moore used thumb and fingers on his right hand instead of the more conventional flatpick. He put a thumbpick on his thumb to help him damp the bass string notes (which people now associate with Chet Atkins), as well as to produce a stronger attack on doublestops and chords — which he almost always strummed downwards, bass to treble. Unlike some lead guitarists, Scotty didn't rest his ring or little finger on the body of the guitar.

Scotty Moore was an experienced guitarist by the time he was called upon to produce accompaniment and solos for the early Elvis material, so he was able to bring to bear the battery of skills that he had acquired over the years. He used partial chords, doublestops and single notes in his playing, most of which involved a mix of country and blues scales. Unlike many modern guitarists, Scotty didn't play flash "100 mile an hour" solos, but produced well-crafted and melodic riffs and breaks. He used reasonably orthodox left hand fingering, though — in common with many self-taught players — he favoured his 3rd finger when the 4th would be the natural finger to use.

# READING STANDARD & TABLATURE NOTATION

All the material in this book involves 4 beats per bar. It will help you to follow the notation if you learn the different note lengths:

| Note | Rest | | | | |
|------|------|---|---|---|---|
| o | ▬ | = | semibreve | = | 4 beats |
| ♩ (minim) | ▬ | = | minim | = | 2 beats |
| ♩ | 𝄽 | = | crotchet | = | 1 beat |
| ♪ | 𝄾 | = | quaver | = | ½ beat | ( ♫ = 2 quavers = 1 beat) |
| ♬ | 𝄿 | = | semiquaver | = | ¼ beat | ( ♬♬ = 4 semiquavers = 1 beat) |

When a dot is placed after a note or rest, its length is increased by half again i.e. ♩. = 1½ beats. Where a curved line joins two notes of the same pitch, add the two note lengths together.

Tablature is a system where 6 lines represent the 6 strings of the guitar. The top line is the string with the highest pitch — the thinnest, 1st string. The numbers on the lines/strings indicate the fret position to be held down by the left hand and played by the right. (Because notes of the same pitch can usually be played in different places on the fretboard, this is useful for giving a clear and immediate location for each note.)

Tablature normally doesn't tell you which left or right hand fingers to use, though some guidance can be given above or below the notation. To help you follow the material in this book more easily, I've given fingering and other notes after each piece. The warm-up pieces also have some indications below the notation.

Here is a two-bar sample of standard and tablature notation together, as used in this book:

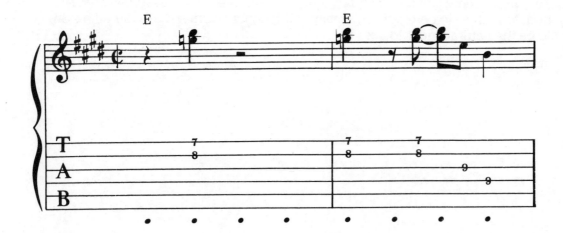

The notes and rests of the standard music notation are EXACTLY in line with the tablature notes and beats — tap your foot on these beats (shown by the four dots) and count the rhythm as indicated.

The underlying chord of each bar is shown above the standard notation. In the first bar, tap your foot on the 1st beat and play nothing. On the 2nd beat play two notes at the same time — the B at the 7th fret of the 1st string and the G (a bluesy, flattened 3rd note) at the 8th fret of the 2nd string. Use your 1st & 2nd left hand fingers and either strum down across the two strings with a flatpick or thumbpick, like Scotty Moore, or use thumb/index or even index and middle fingers. Stop the note after a beat/crotchet by releasing the pressure on the strings, and tap your foot on the 3rd & 4th beats of that bar. The next bat involves the same two notes for the 1st beat, stopped again after a crotchet. Then tap your foot on the 2nd beat and play the B & G notes again on the half beat, holding those till halfway through the 3rd beat. Then put your 3rd & 4th left hand fingers down for the E & low B notes, counting "&4".

¢ means "cut time". With this time signature, the tempo will be fast or very fast, and the 1st & 3rd beats will be stressed more than the others.

# THE SCOTTY MOORE GUITAR EMBELLISHMENTS

Embellishments are necessary for variety, dynamics and "attack" in lead guitar playing. Like other lead guitarists, Scotty Moore employs a number of special guitar techniques or embellishments when constructing his riffs and solos.

### The Hammer-on

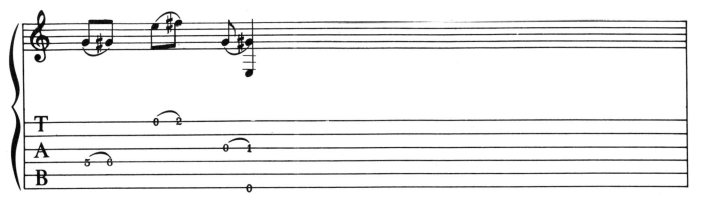

A curved line from a lower pitched note to a higher note means the left hand does a hammer-on. The left-hand finger comes down firmly onto the string to produce a second note after the right hand has struck the first. This could be from a lower to a higher fretted note, as in the first example above — the 1st finger is placed at the 5th fret of the 4th string and the right hand strikes it. Then the 2nd finger comes down onto the 6th fret to produce a second note. A hammer-on can be from an open string to a fretted note, as in the second example. In the third example, the right hand thumb must strike the open 6th string *at the same time* as the 1st finger of the left hand comes down onto the 1st fret of the 3rd string — this is a favourite technique of Scotty Moore when playing in the alternating thumb style, as you'll see.

### The Pull-off

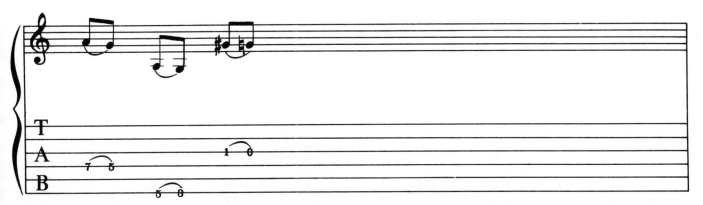

The same curved line is drawn to indicate a pull-off. This is in a sense the opposite of a hammer-on. The left hand produces a second note that is lower in pitch then the first. The name comes from the fact that the finger must pull the string slightly before coming off — to make the note loud enough. Where the second note is fretted, the left hand finger, usually the first, must be in place when the first note is struck.

### The Slide

6    When a slide is performed, the left hand produces a second note, like the hammer-on and pull-off. The slide can go up or down the fretboard as shown in the first two examples. Scotty Moore quite often slides two or three notes at the same time, as in the third and fifth examples. Because there is no specific fret number shown before the slide in these cases, just slide from any lower fret that feels right — the slide should be very quick. The fourth example above involves a wavy line — this means you should slide your finger down along the string and off at *any* fret. The bracketed numbers in the last example mean that the slide is done as usual to that fret and then the right hand immediately strikes the strings *again* as soon as the left hand reaches the new position.

**The Bend**

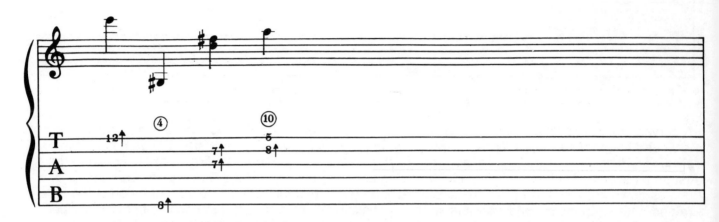

A bend is where the left hand increases the pitch of a note by pushing the string across the guitar neck. This is indicated in tablature in this book by a small arrow after the fret number — which shows where the left hand playing finger is placed. When a string is bent only slightly — below a semitone or fret — then just an arrow is shown (as in the first example). If a string is bent up in pitch by one or more semitones, a circled fret number is given above. This is the true pitch of the bent note, which is also shown in the standard music notation — as in the second and fourth examples. Sometimes two strings are bent together, as in the third example, but occasionally two strings are played and only one is bent — in the last example above, both notes are the same pitch of A. In all cases, Scotty Moore bends the notes quickly.

**Multiple Embellishments**

Scotty Moore will sometimes produce more than one extra note with his left hand after the right hand has struck the string for the first note. The first example involves the 2nd finger hammering on to the 6th fret of the 4th string after the 5th fret G note (fingered by the 1st finger of the left hand) has been struck by the right hand, followed by the 3rd finger hammering on to the 7th fret. The second example involves a hammer-on followed by a pull-off. The 1st finger holds the G note and the 3rd hammers on and pulls off one after the other. Occasionally Scotty does three extra notes with his left hand — as in the third example. Use all four left hand fingers here. The last example of multiple embellishments has to be done with the volume of the guitar well up — there are four slides one after the other, followed by a pull-off, i.e. five extra notes! Use your 1st finger. This is from "Any Way You Want Me".

## Damping

All lead guitarists use the damping technique to control the length of notes as well as to produce more variety of sound and "attack" in their playing. The left hand releases its pressure on the string, but still keeps in contact with it — thus stopping the string from ringing on. The right hand fingers or palm can also be used to stop notes from ringing on — or the thumb, see below. Damping is not marked on the tablature in this book, so you need to check the standard music notation to see how long a note should ring — if there's a rest sign after the note, then the note must be damped to some degree. If you can get to listen to the actual recordings of the solos transcribed in this book, this would help you to produce the exact note lengths and sounds.

## The Alternating Thumb Style & Damping

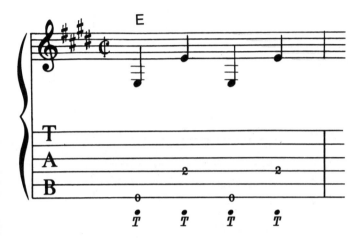

Scotty Moore uses a thumbpick on his right hand thumb. This enables him to lower the heel of his right hand on to the bass strings and still strike the strings easily when playing in the alternating thumb style (alternating bass notes are shown above). The heel of the right hand damps the bass string notes slightly to produce a springier rhythm — Chet Atkins is renowned for this technique.

## The Swing Rhythm

Much of the music in this book should be played with a "swing" i.e. notes between beats should be delayed until just before the following beat. You'll see this sign at the start of the notation when the music should be played with a swing: ♪ᶾ♪ . This means that when there are two quavers in a beat, you should make the first one twice as long as the second.

When the music is swung, the underlying pulse is *three equal notes* per beat i.e. triplet quavers, so you can expect to see some of these in the solos that involve a swing rhythm. Make sure all three quavers are the same length. To make it clear for you, here is a bar of quavers in a straight rhythm, with a bar of swung quavers beneath, plus a bar of triplet quavers beneath them:

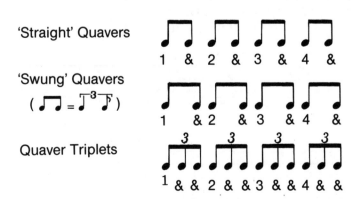

In the solos that involve a swing rhythm you'll come across many bars which include both swung quavers and triplet quavers. Work out the rhythm very carefully before playing them.

# TYPICAL SCOTTY MOORE RIFFS

Here are a selection of the type of guitar riffs Scotty Moore used on the Elvis Presley songs included in this book, and other material. Notes on left and right hand fingering and choice of scales are given after each example. Read these carefully to help you reproduce the riffs correctly.

**Chordal Riffs**

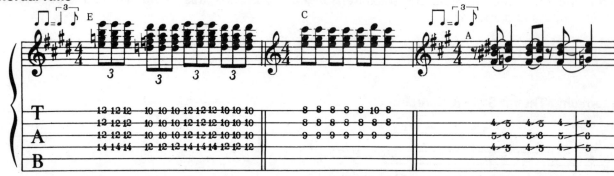

Scotty often uses chordal riffs with partial chords. The first example involves this shape at the 12th then 10th fret:

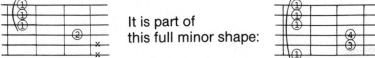

It is part of this full minor shape:

The underlying chord for the bar, as shown, is E major. The use of partial minor chords produces a bluesy effect. The second example involves a partial shape from the C major at the 8th fret, while the third involves part of a 7th chord slid from the 4th to 5th fret:

You can do downstrums across these chords, or pluck with thumb and fingers.

**Doublestops**

Instead of three or four note chords, Scotty often uses "doublestops" i.e. two notes at a time. The first example involves the root and 5th of the E chord (E & B) followed by the flattened 3rd & 5th (G & B). Do downstrums with your right hand for all of these, with thumbpick or flatpick. Or you could use the 1st & 2nd fingers. The doublestops in the second example are a 6th apart — F to D. The F natural is a flattened 7th and gives a bluesy sound. Use your thumb and 2nd finger on the right hand.

Two notes of the usual A chord at the 5th fret are used in the first example above. Slide the left hand up from any fret. The second example involves part of an A7 shape, then part of an E major shape. Scotty plays them all with downstrums of his thumbpick.

**Bass Lines**

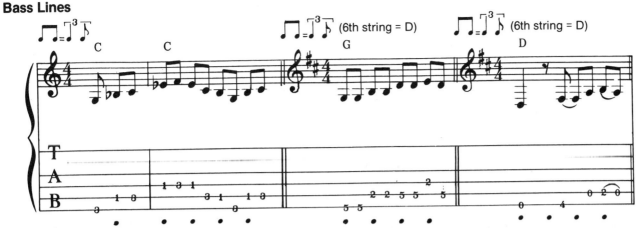

As well as the more usual treble note riffs, Scotty is also capable of producing raunchy and exciting bass lines. The first example is from "Hound Dog", the second from "Jailhouse Rock", and the last (repeated four times) is the introduction to "Don't Be Cruel". Tune your 6th string down a tone to D for the last two. Use your 1st & 3rd fingers of your left hand for all of them, though the orthodox fingering for the second example would be the 1st & 4th fingers. Alternate your thumb and index fingers on the right hand — or do downstrokes on the beat and up off the beat with a pick. Scotty would have used his thumbpick. Notice the use of the flattened 3rd & 7th notes of the C major scale in the first example, to produce a bluesy feel.

**The Alternating Thumb Style**

Scotty Moore, like Chet Atkins, is a master of the alternating thumb style with a damped bass. Use a thumbpick and drop the heel of your right hand down on the bass strings near the bridge to muffle the sound slightly. You could also use the alternating thumb patterns successfully without damping the bass string notes. Scotty used the alternating thumb style for a fuller rhythm behind Elvis's vocals and at the end of breaks. He often used shapes up and down the fretboard — hold the usual open E chord for the first example, but move up the fretboard for the second example:

**Trills**

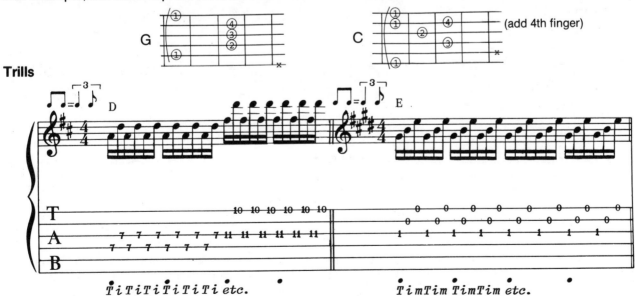

On slow ballads, Scotty liked to do occasional trills. These songs involve a slow triplet tempo, and he would normally do 6 semiquavers to a beat as shown, using the thumb and index finger on his right hand. Alternate them rapidly to produce the correct fast and smooth sound — listen to "I'll Never Let You Go" and "I Forgot To Remember To Forget Her" to hear the original sound.

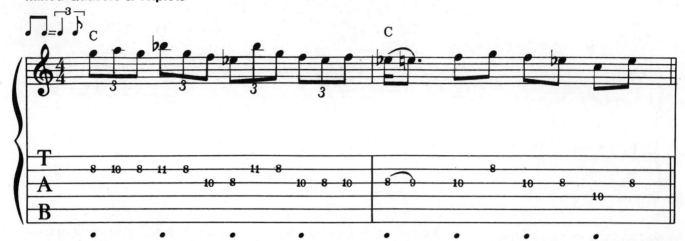

Swung Quavers plus triplet quavers are very common in Scotty's solos. This example comes from "When It Rains It Really Pours" (The Complete Sun Sessions double L.P.). Hold a bar with your 1st finger across the 2nd & 3rd strings at the 8th fret, and add your 2nd, 3rd & 4th fingers for the other notes. Notice the use of both C major scale notes *and* flattened "blue" notes.

### Mixed Triplets & Semiquavers

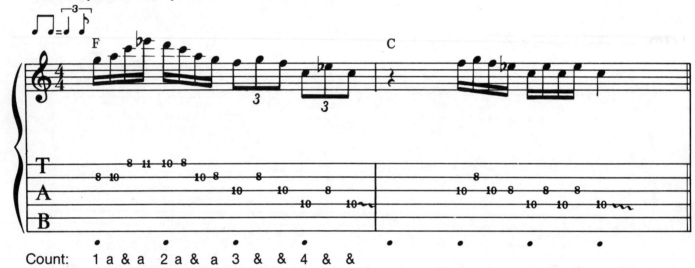

Count:    1 a & a  2 a & a  3 & & 4 & &

Scotty Moore usually kept his solos simple (as directed by Sam Phillips of Sun Records), but he occasionally slipped in pushes against the rhythm — like the semiquavers in the bars above (again from "When It Rains It Really Pours"). Hold a bar across the top three strings with your 1st finger, but be careful counting the rhythm — switching from four semiquavers per beat to triplets is tricky.

### Chromatic Runs

Occasional forays into chromatic notes can spice up some solos — the first example is from "Too Much" which you'll find later in this book. Here I've transposed it into the simpler key of A major. Use your little finger then others in the 2nd position, then move to the 4th position. The right hand can alternate down and up strokes with a flatpick or thumb and flatpick or just thumbpick like Scotty Moore. Or you could do down/up/down strokes for each triplet. The second example is from "Just Because" (The Complete Sun Sessions double L.P.). Start with your 2nd & 3rd fingers and switch the 1st for the 2nd and then move it back one fret. Use your thumb, index and middle fingers on your right hand.

# SCOTTY'S BOOGIE

Music by RUSS SHIPTON

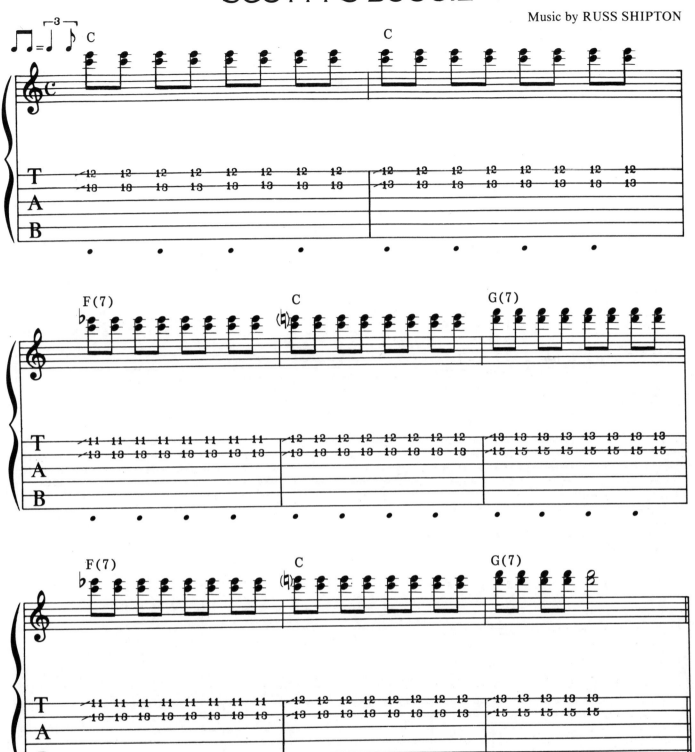

### Notes On "Scotty's Boogie"

♩ = 108. This piece should be played at a moderate tempo i.e. 108 crotchets or beats should be played over a period of one minute. This means you tap your foot about 1½ times per second.

Simple "doublestops" (two notes played together) are used here. For all the chords you play just two of the chord notes i.e. C & E for the C chord, C & E♭ (the flattened 7th) for the F chord, and D & F (the flattened 7th) for the G chord:

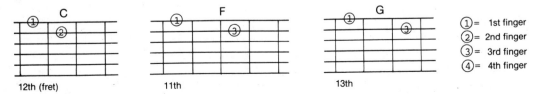

Swing the rhythm by delaying the notes between the beats a little. Try changing key to use the same ideas in other positions — move down three frets for the key of A for example.

# BLUEBERRY PIE

Music by RUSS SHIPTON

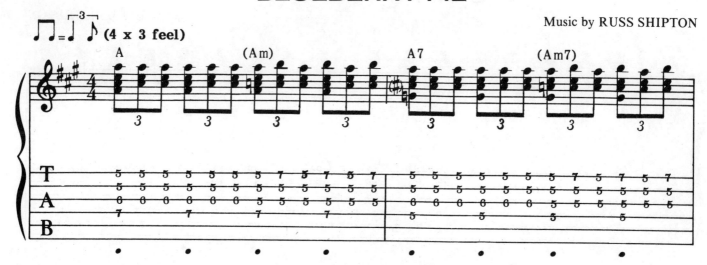

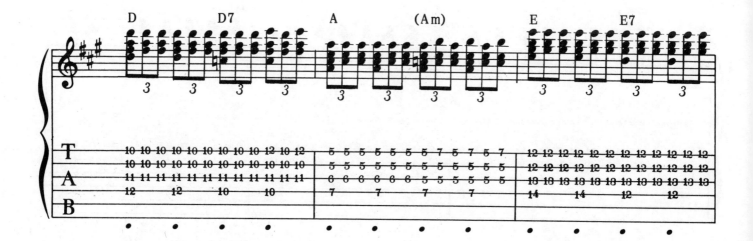

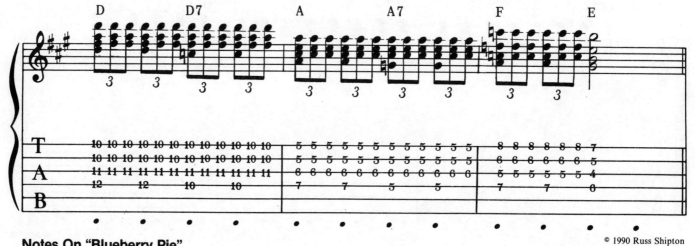

© 1990 Russ Shipton

## Notes On "Blueberry Pie"

♩ = 80. Because of the continuous triplets, this piece must be played at a slowish tempo. Count 123, 123 etc. and tap your foot on each beat.

By playing 7th and minor chords against the underlying chords of the sequence, a bluesy feel is produced. Add your 4th finger to these shapes when required:

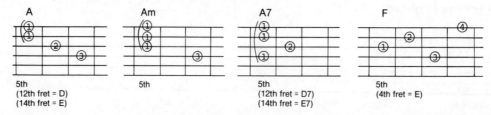

Play the bass notes with your thumb and pluck the treble strings with your index, middle and ring fingers on your right hand. Should you prefer to use a flatpick, strum down/up/down for each triplet group.

# FOLLOW THAT CHORD

Music by RUSS SHIPTON

## Notes On "Follow That Chord"

♩ = 152. This lead solo should eventually be played quite fast.

Some lead players tend to follow chord changes quite closely, while others use a "blanket" approach — see the piece "Blanket Lead" later. This piece will give you some ideas about adapting riffs for different underlying chords. Bar across the first two or three strings with your left hand 1st finger and add your 4th (or 3rd) finger for the flattened 7th note:

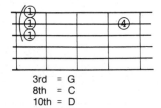

3rd = G
8th = C
10th = D

Bar across the 3rd fret for the G chord riff, the 8th fret for the D riff, and the 10th fret for the C.

After swinging the rhythm, try playing the solo with a straight rhythm (see my notes on page 7). You could also try making the sequence into a more common 12-bar one by adding some bars. A 12-bar blues sequence in the key of G would include these bars: G G G G C C G G D C G D.

# CHET'S WALK

Music by RUSS SHIPTON

## Notes On "Chet's Walk"

♩ = 208. This piece is written in cut time and eventually should be played quite fast. In cut time there is normally a stronger stress on the 1st & 3rd beats of each bar. Play this solo slowly to start with until you get the flow of the right hand thumb bouncing from one bass string to the other. This piece is NOT SWUNG, so the notes between beats are played *exactly* halfway between them.

Here are the positions for your left hand to hold:

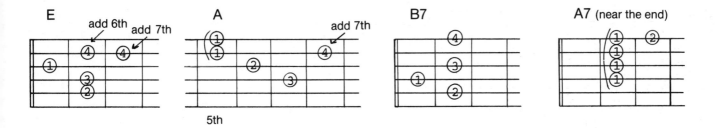

The 6th & 7th notes, added with your little finger, should not be allowed to ring on very long — release the pressure on the string. The right hand heel can "damp" the bass notes slightly by resting on the bass strings near the bridge. Using a thumbpick may help you to do this more easily. Chet Atkins is one of the foremost players of this alternating thumb damped bass style. Read my notes on page 7 for a fuller explanation of the technique involved.

# THE FOURTH MAN THEME

Music by RUSS SHIPTON

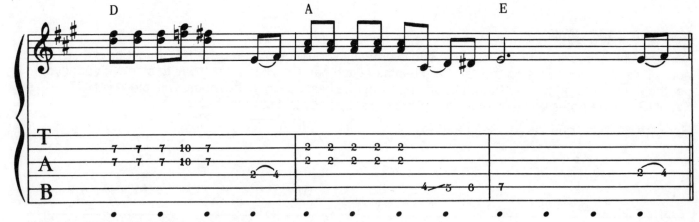

**Notes On "The Fourth Man Theme"**

♩ = 112. Play this piece at a moderate speed.

This solo shows how Scotty Moore might use partial chord shapes to produce a simple but effective lead break. Like the last piece, the left hand follows the chord changes:

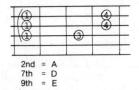

Add the 3rd & 4th fingers where required.

2nd = A
7th = D
9th = E

The 1st finger is covering part of this more recognisable chord shape:

You can use your right hand thumb for the bass notes and 1st & 2nd fingers for the trebles. Play this piece *without* a swing.

# MOORE RHYTHM

Music by RUSS SHIPTON

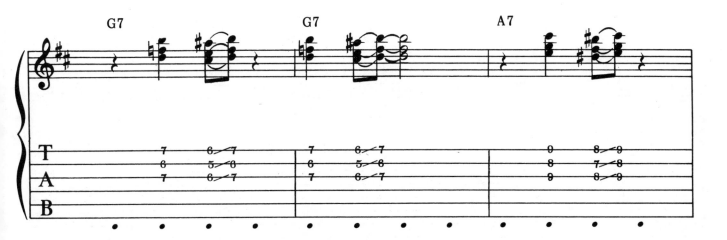

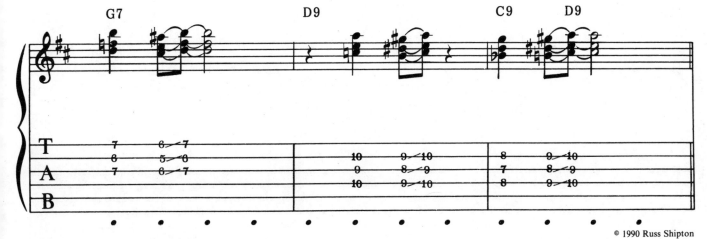

**Notes On "Moore Rhythm"**

♩ = 138. This piece should be played reasonably fast once you've learnt the syncopated rhythm pattern. Swing the rhythm.

The left hand is holding simple jazz-style shapes that Scotty often used for a section of his solos. Sliding from one fret down produces an interesting rhythm and sense of movement. You'll notice a B♯ note in bar 5 — that is played as a C note, as you'll see from the tablature. Here are the shapes and fingering required:

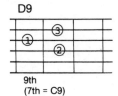

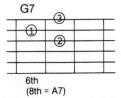

Damp (i.e. stop) the notes when a rest is shown after them in the standard notation. You can make this into a 12-bar sequence by adding some bars as you did for the previous piece: D9 D9 D9 D9 G7 G7 D9 D9 A7 G7 D9 D9.

# ELVIS BLUES

Music by RUSS SHIPTON

## Notes On "Elvis Blues"

♩ = 112. Eventually this should be played at a moderate tempo, but take each bar very slowly to begin with.

In the first five bars your left hand stays in the "8th position" i.e. with the 1st finger covering the 8th fret notes, the 2nd finger the 9th fret and so on. Use your *2nd* finger for the last note of beat 1 bar 6, and slide up to the 12th fret. Your left hand is then in the "11th position", until sliding back down in a similar way at the end of bar 7.

Notice Scotty's use of the bluesy flattened 3rd and flattened 7th notes — in the standard music notation these are easy to see because of natural or sharp/flat signs placed next to them.

You could use a flatpick for this solo, or a thumbpick like Scotty Moore. Alternate down and upstrokes, generally doing downstrokes on the beat. Either strum across doublestops or pluck them with thumb and index of your right hand. Experiment to see which fingering you feel more comfortable with.

# BLANKET LEAD

Music by RUSS SHIPTON

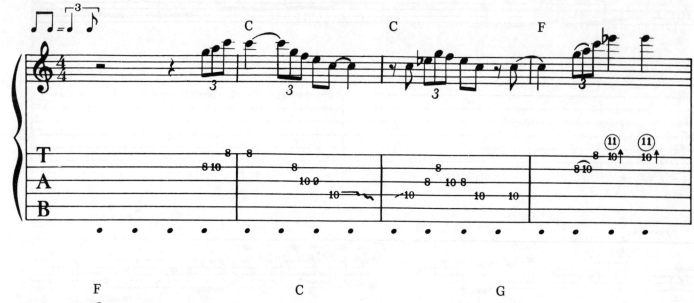

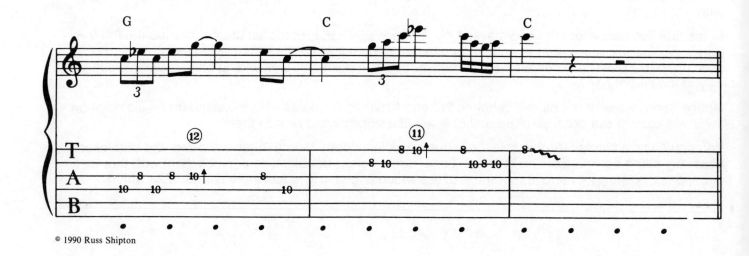

## Notes On "Blanket Lead"

♩ = 96. This solo should be played at a slow to medium speed.

In this piece your left hand plays a "blanket" lead style, i.e. it stays in one position throughout, rather than move around the fretboard following the chord changes. Hold your 1st finger over the 8th fret, 2nd over the 9th and so on. Count each bar carefully after working out what your fingers have to do. Check what is involved with the embellishments at the start of the book where they are explained. Remember that a rest after a note in the standard music notation means you have to damp the string. The penultimate bar has *four* notes on the last beat i.e. semiquavers. Because this piece has a swing rhythm, semiquavers "cut across" the rhythm a little. They are also hard to squeeze into one beat in time!

The bend in bar 8 is a two-fret (one tone) bend — if you haven't got an unwound 3rd string, this could be difficult. Place your 1st & 2nd fingers behind the 3rd finger, then they can help with the bend.

# (YOU'RE SO SQUARE) BABY I DON'T CARE

Words and Music by JERRY LEIBER & MIKE STOLLER

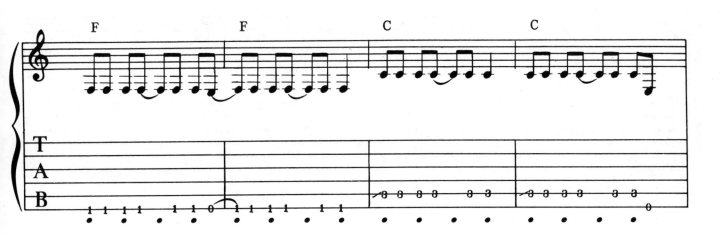

## Notes On "Baby I Don't Care"

♩ = 188. This means the song is fast. The lead break is in the "Duane Eddy" bass style, and though quite simple, it is very effective with a little reverb. on the sound. Don't stop the notes except in the last two bars.

Use your left hand 3rd finger for the C notes and the 1st finger for the F notes. Use the 2nd finger for the F♯ notes and then move your 1st finger to the 3rd fret for the G notes in the last two bars, adding the 3rd finger for the A notes.

Do downstrokes on the beat notes and upstrokes on those between beats. Swing the rhythm by delaying the notes between beats slightly.

# BLUE MOON OF KENTUCKY

Words and Music by BILL MONROE

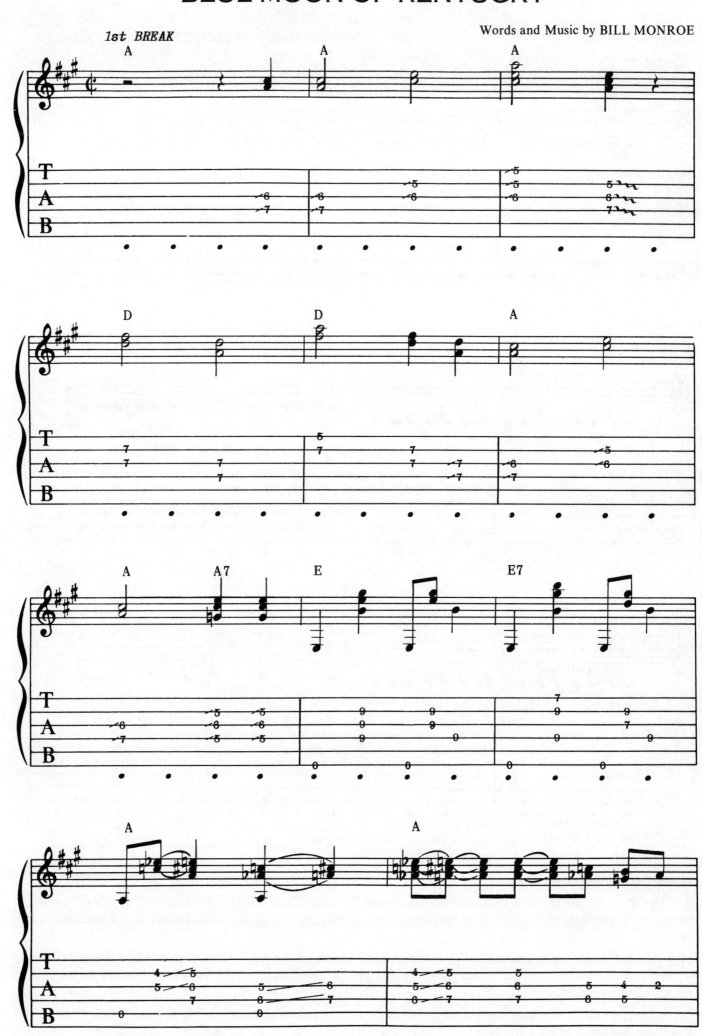

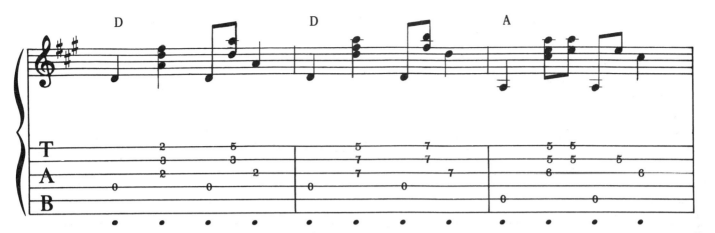

## Notes On "Blue Moon Of Kentucky"

♩ = 220. This song is fast. Stress the first and third beats of each bar a little.

This break starts with doublestops and partial chords, and continues with a full right hand style — the "alternating thumb" pattern. See page 7. The A bars are based on this shape:

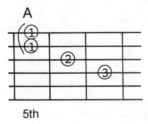

The E & D shapes are like this:

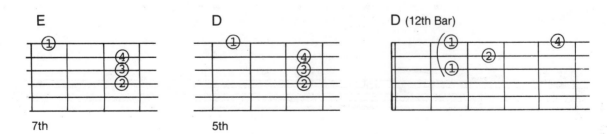

You can use just two fingers for the first seven bars, rather than the whole shape. Use your thumb and index or middle finger on your right hand.

# BLUE SUEDE SHOES

Words and Music by CARL LEE PERKINS

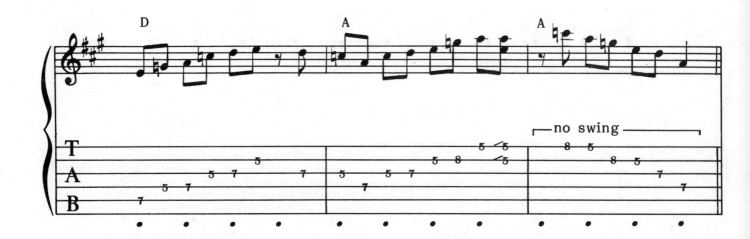

### Notes On "Blue Suede Shoes"

♩ = 184. This piece is played at a fast tempo.

This solo is a prime example of "blanket" lead playing. Scotty stays in the middle of the fretboard throughout both breaks — your left hand is held in the "5th position":

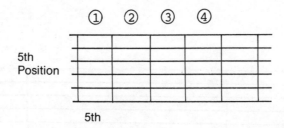

Start by sliding a two-string bar with your 1st finger — these kinds of slides are done very quickly. In fact, you could hold a small bar across two or more strings at the 5th fret for the whole solo, adding your 2nd, 3rd and 4th fingers for the 6th, 7th and 8th fret notes. In these breaks Scotty uses notes from the A major scale, apart from the 3rd and 7th notes which he flattens for a bluesy effect i.e. C and G natural. There are several "multiple embellishments" in this solo — see my notes on page 6.

Scotty probably strums across the doublestops with his thumbpick, but you could use a flatpick or thumb and index on your right hand. When using a pick, it is usual to strum down on the beat notes and up on the offbeat.

This song involves a swing rhythm, so delay the notes between beats a little. Notice that the notes in the last bar of the second break are played *without* a swing i.e. you should play the notes between beats *exactly* halfway between beats. This means they cut across the underlying swing rhythm, producing a slightly jarring, but effective syncopation.

# HARBOUR LIGHTS

Words and Music by JIMMY KENNEDY and HUGH WILLIAMS

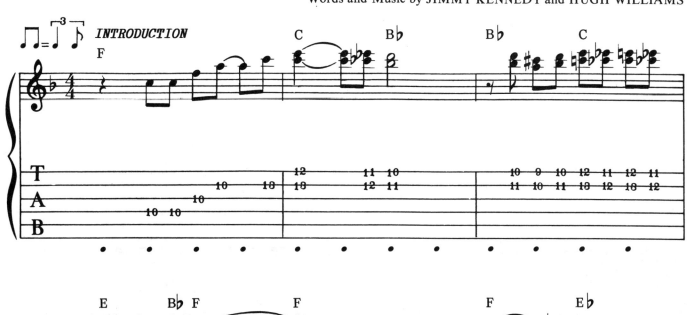

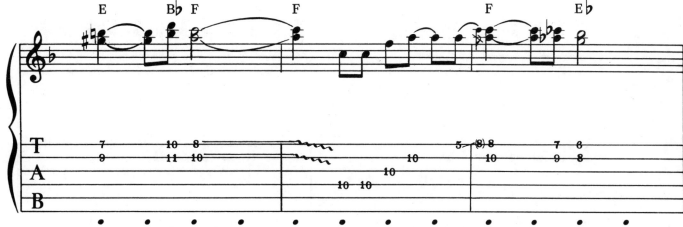

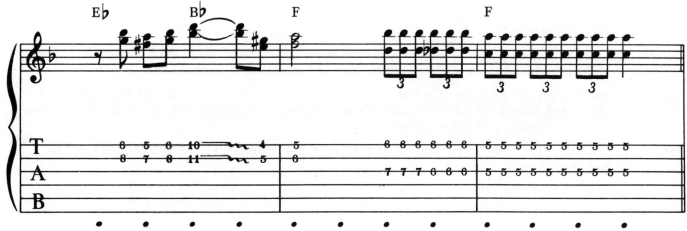

## Notes On "Harbour Lights"

♩ = 76. This is a ballad and is played quite slowly.

The key of F major is straightforward if you understand your doublestop scale. Start with a short bar across the 2nd, 3rd & 4th strings at the 10th fret (a partial F chord). Then use your 2nd & 3rd fingers for the doublestops in the following two bars. (Use your 1st instead of 2nd finger for the E & F doublestops in the 4th bar.) Hold the A & C notes in bar 4 for 2½ beats, then slide off any fret below at the end of the third. The slide from bar 5 to bar 6 means the right hand strikes again — see my notes on page 6.

Use some vibrato for these kinds of "moody" solos — shake your left hand from side to side to sustain the notes.

Sometimes you'll come across C♭ in the music notation — this is played as a B note.

# HEARTBREAK HOTEL

Words and Music by MAE BOREN AXTON, TOMMY DURDEN and ELVIS PRESLEY

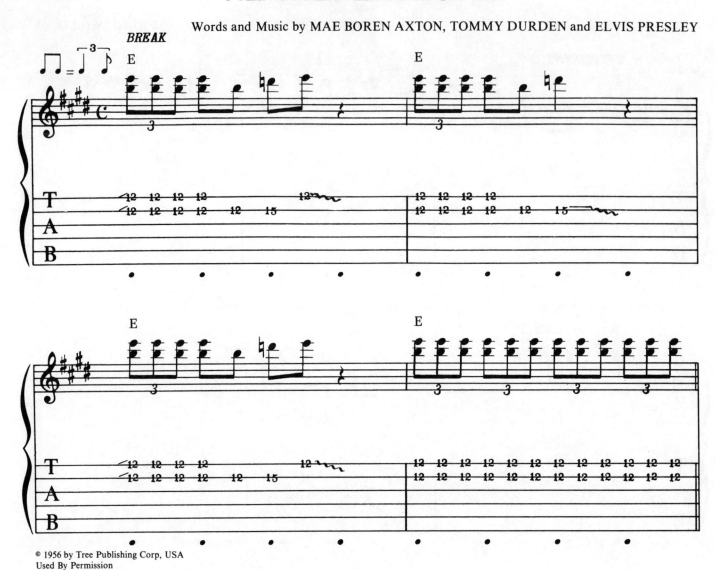

### Notes On "Heartbreak Hotel"

♩ = 90. This solo should be played at a slow to moderate pace. The pitch of the song is given as the key of E major, but the original record is actually a little below E in standard tuning.

Bar across the top two strings at the 12th fret with your 1st finger, and add your 3rd or 4th finger for the D natural note. Scotty Moore will have done all downstrums across the doublestops with his thumbpick, but you could use a flatpick or thumb and index finger.

Make sure you make the triplets of equal length, and swing the notes between beats where there are only two notes in the beat.

# HOUND DOG

Words and Music by JERRY LEIBER and MIKE STOLLER

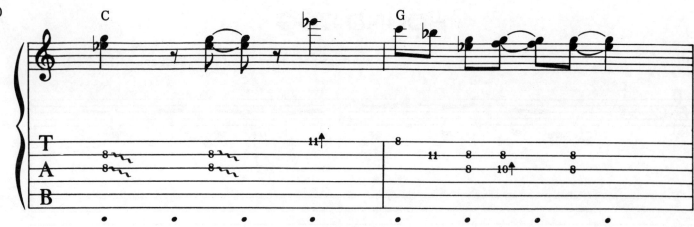

## Notes On "Hound Dog"

♩ = 174. This piece is reasonably fast.

Here Scotty starts the break with a dynamic and exciting bass riff which includes the bluesy flattened 7th note, B♭. He then works his way up the fretboard in bars 4 & 5 to the 8th position. Use your 1st finger for the C note in bar 4. The 3rd finger does a quick slide to the 7th fret, and the 2nd finger frets the E note at the 9th fret of the 3rd string.

The slides that come off at any fret provide a great dynamic effect — try to listen to the original to hear the exact sound created.

# I BEG OF YOU

Words and Music by ROSE MARIE McCOT and KELLY OWENS

**Notes On "I Beg Of You"**

♩ = 157. This song is reasonably fast.

Producing effective riffs between vocal lines, and creating exciting and appropriate introductions and endings, is often the job of the lead guitarist. Here I've transcribed the introduction and various riffs from "I Beg Of You". The key is E♭ major, so should you want to feel more comfortable with the notes take them all down by one fret — then you're in the more familiar key of D.

The B♭♭ notes (B double flat) in the key of E♭ should be played as A notes.

Don't forget to swing the rhythm by delaying the notes between beats.

# I DON'T CARE IF THE SUN DON'T SHINE

Words and Music by MACK DAVID

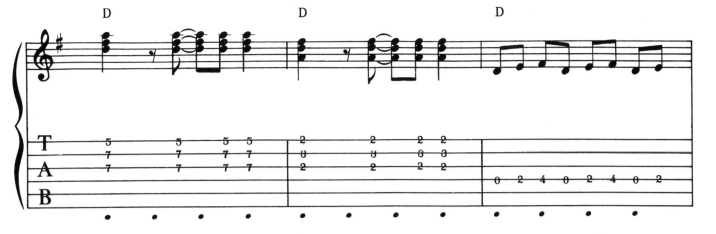

### Notes On "I Don't Care If The Sun Don't Shine"

♩ = 224. The cut-time rhythm make the music easier to follow, but the beats are played very fast. When the tempo is fast, the swing feel may not be so obvious, but you must still remember the underlying triplets.

In the first few bars of the break, Scotty moves down gradually from the G in the 10th position (two notes of the A shape) to the G in the 3rd position (two notes of the E shape). On the way he adds the flattened 3rd B♭ note. In bar 6 you should hold a fuller G chord for the alternating thumb pattern:

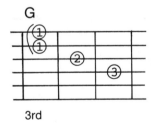

3rd

In the middle bars of the break, various D chord shapes are used — sometimes with the added 9th E note:

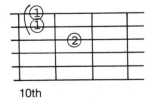

10th

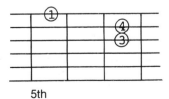

5th

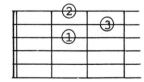

There is a rest following the first chord of bars 10-14, so these should be damped.

# I FORGOT TO REMEMBER TO FORGET HER

Words and Music by CHARLIE FEATHERS and STANLEY KESSLER

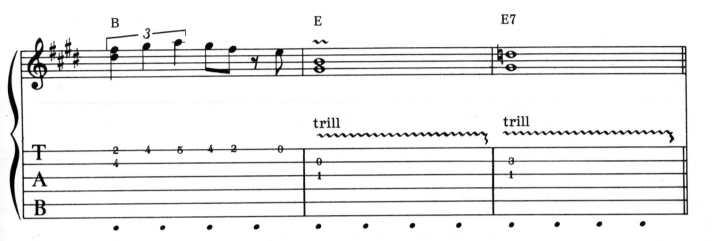

## Notes On "I Forgot To Remember To Forgot Her"

♩ = 110. This is a slow to moderate ballad.

Like the last song, this breaks involves doublestops — but this time in the key of E major. Here again, Scotty is moving from one to another position of the same chord. Use your 1st & 3rd or 1st & 2nd fingers.

The trills are the only difficult aspect about this solo. Alternate your thumb and 1st finger rapidly, playing six notes per beat. See my notes on page 6, but also try to listen to the original recording to fully appreciate the smooth and flowing, slightly laid back sound that Scotty gets.

# I GOT A SWEETIE (I GOT A WOMAN)

Words and Music by RAY CHARLES

## Notes On "I Got A Woman"

♩ = 235. This should be played at an extremely fast tempo, but obviously you'll need to work up to the correct speed gradually. This piece is played *without a swing*.

Scotty Moore uses the alternating thumb style for the whole of this break. you can try damping the bass strings once you can play the notes in the usual way — see my notes about the alternating thumb style and damping on page 7.

Here are the shapes you should hold with your left hand for this solo:

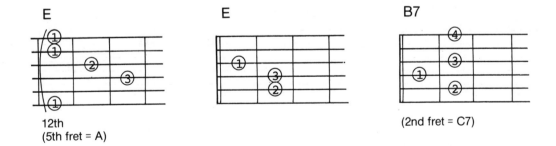

Add the 4th finger for the 6th & 7th notes. Stop these added notes short i.e. keep them to about a quaver or half beat in length.

Notice that this piece has a 16-bar format. You'll come across 8-bar, 12-bar, 16-bar and 24-bar sequences.

# I'M LEFT, YOU'RE RIGHT, SHE'S GONE

Words and Music by STANLEY A KESLER and WILLIAM E TAYLOR

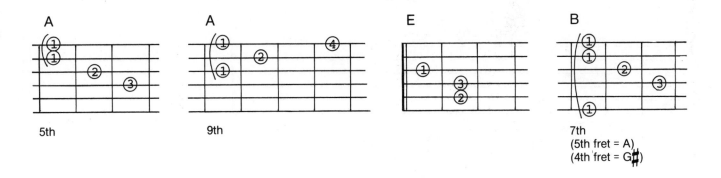

### Notes On "I'm Left, You're Right, She's Gone"

♩ = 180. This is another cut-time rhythm with a fast tempo — with a swing this time.

Scotty starts this break with doublestops from the E & B chords, then switches to the alternating thumb style — see my notes on this style and damping the bass strings on page 7. Here are the shapes you need to hold with your left hand (add the 4th finger for the 6th notes):

A

5th

A

9th

E

B

7th
(5th fret = A)
(4th fret = G♯)

# JAILHOUSE ROCK

Words and Music by JERRY LEIBER and MIKE STOLLER

6th String = D    *Boogie (behind voice from bar 9-16 each verse)*

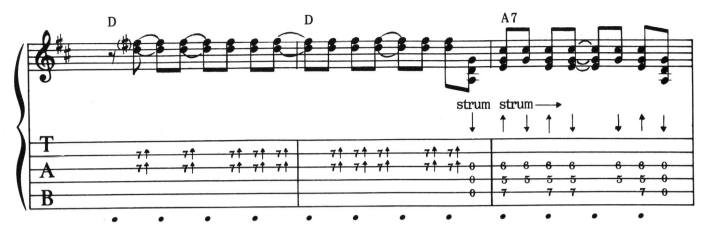

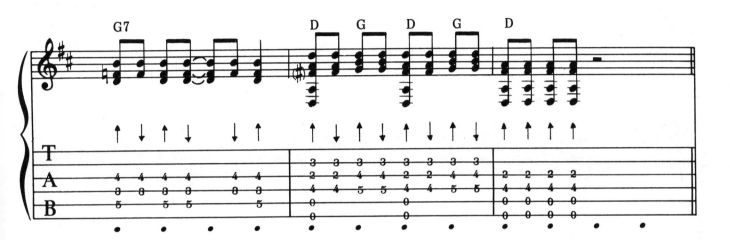

## Notes On "Jailhouse Rock"

♩ = 168. This song is played quite fast. For some reason, the boogie guitar part behind the voice — given first above — is played with very little swing feel, yet the lead break has a definite swing.

You'll need to tune your 6th string down to D for this solo — it should sound an octave below the pitch of your 4th string.

Hold these shapes for the last four bars:

A7

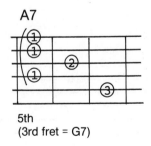

5th
(3rd fret = G7)

D

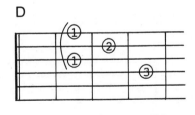

G

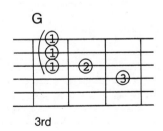

3rd

# LAWDY MISS CLAWDY

Words and Music by LLOYD PRICE

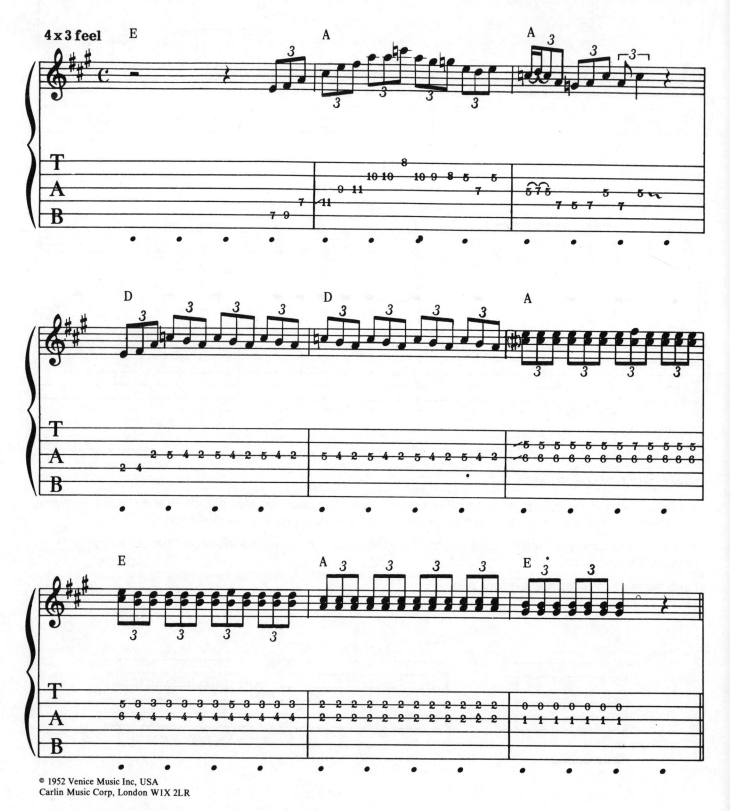

## Notes On "Lawdy Miss Clawdy"

♩ = 104. This song is played at a slow to moderate pace, as suggested by the steady stream of triplets. Sometimes you might see this kind of rhythm written in 12/8 time.

Start with your 1st finger on the E note and slide your 3rd finger to the 11th fret. Use your 1st, 4th and 3rd fingers for the runs in bars 4 & 5.

The 1st beat of the 3rd bar involves four notes — the first two are semi-quavers, so are half as long as the quavers. The 3rd beat of bar 3 has just two notes, but rather than being swung, in a sense the opposite happens i.e. the second note is played quickly after the first and is twice as long.

# MEAN WOMAN BLUES

Words and Music by CLAUDE DeMETRUIS

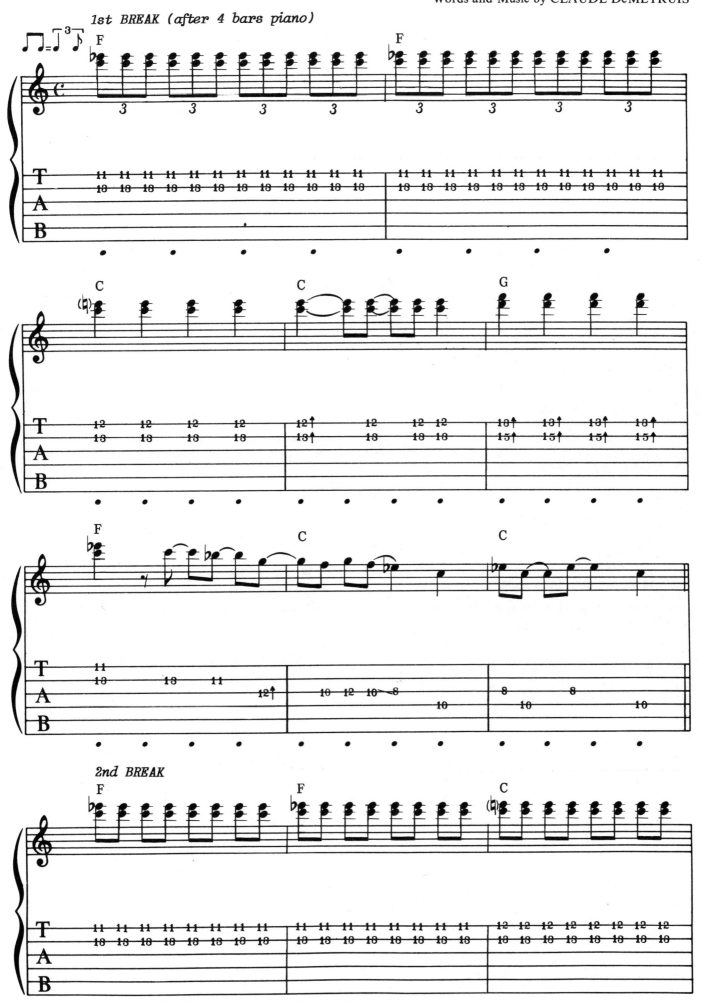

## Notes On "Mean Woman Blues"

♩ = 164. This piece is quite fast, so the opening two bars of triplets have to be played quickly.

Some doublestops are bent slightly in the first break — this creates a slightly bluesy effect as well as varying the sound of the guitar for interest.

Stop the very high C notes quite short in the last two bars. Slide your finger down and off quickly.

# MONEY HONEY

Words and Music by J STONE

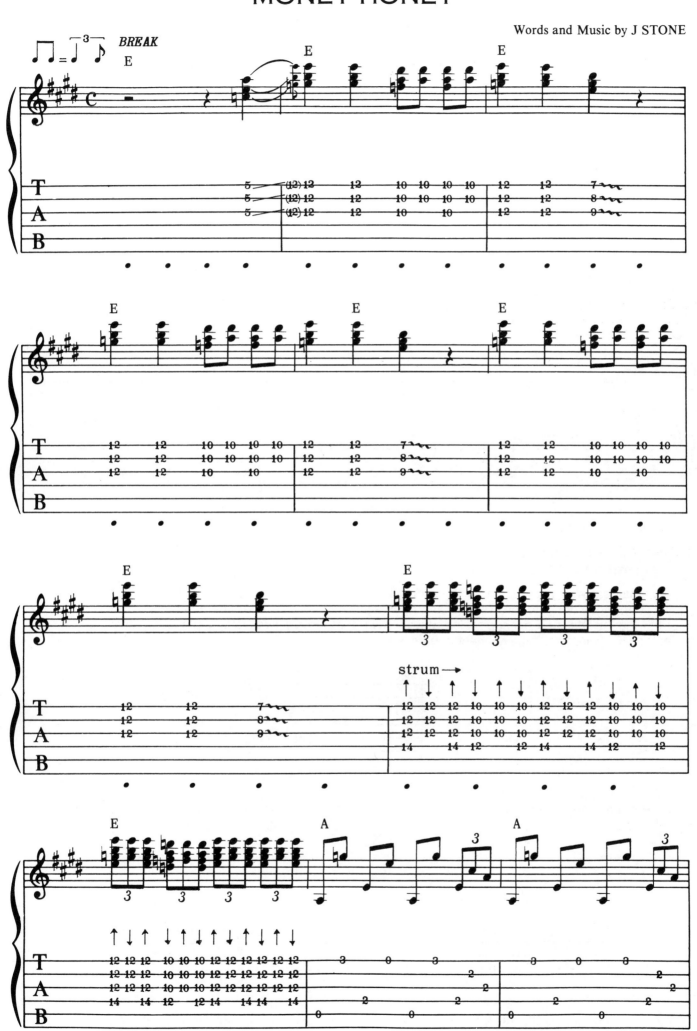

## Notes On "Money Honey"

♩ = 132. The tempo of this piece is quite fast — this means the right hand has to work hard on the triplets in bars 8 & 9.

Slide a small bar with your 1st finger up from the 5th fret to the 12th, and then play the 12th fret notes again. Then move down to the 10th fret and back again to the 12th. The other shape is part of an Em chord at the 7th fret. An Em shape (also moved down temporarily two frets) is played against the underlying E chord for a bluesy effect in bars 8 & 9:

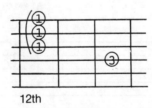

The alternating thumb style takes over from bar 10 (see my notes on page 7), involving these shapes for the left hand:

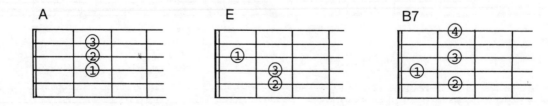

Add your little finger for the 6th & 7th notes. Move your 2nd finger to the 6th string for the F♯ note in the B7 bar.

# MYSTERY TRAIN

Words and Music by SAM C PHILLIPS and HERMAN PARKER, Jr

## Notes On "Mystery Train"

♩ = 240. This is another cut-time song, with an extremely fast beat rate. The rhythm is straight i.e. *without* a swing, and the alternating thumb style is used throughout the break — see page 7.

Here are the chord shapes used by Scotty:

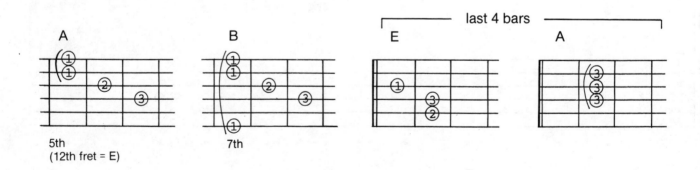

Add your little finger as usual for the 6th & 7th notes. You can use a normal A chord for the last four bars, or drop your 3rd finger down as shown. The A chord notes are stopped short for a jumpy rhythm.

# READY TEDDY

Words and Music by JOHN MARASCALCO and ROBERT BLACKWELL

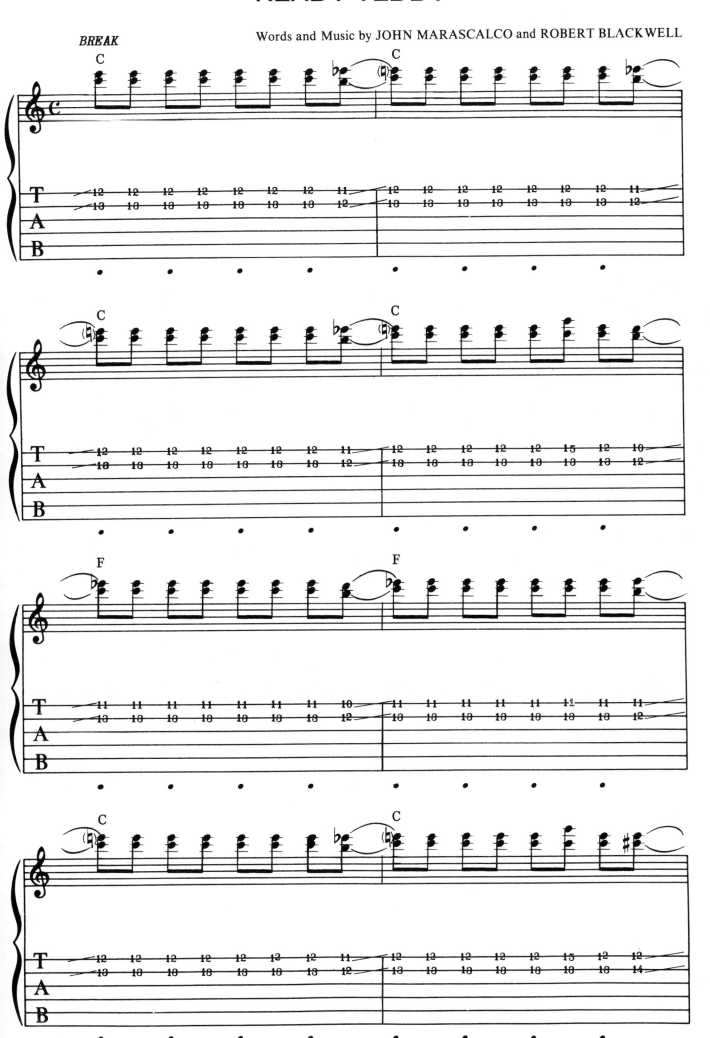

© 1956 Venice Music Inc and Elvis Presley Music Inc, USA
Carlin Music Corp, London W1X 2LR

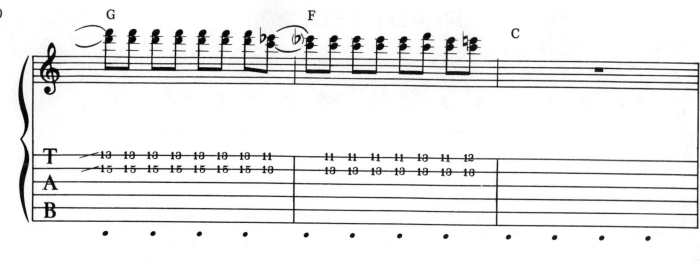

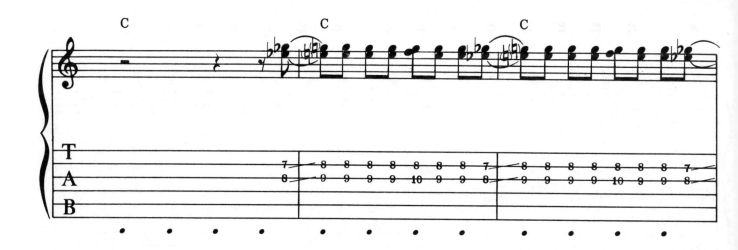

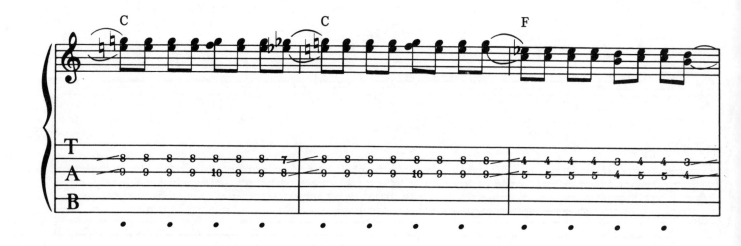

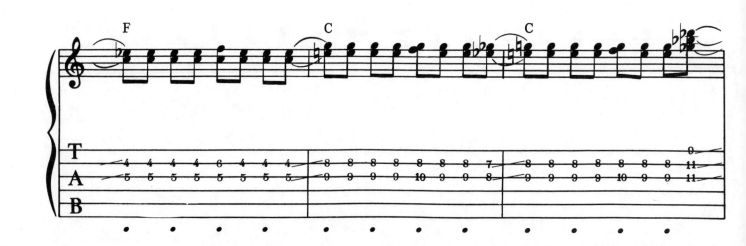

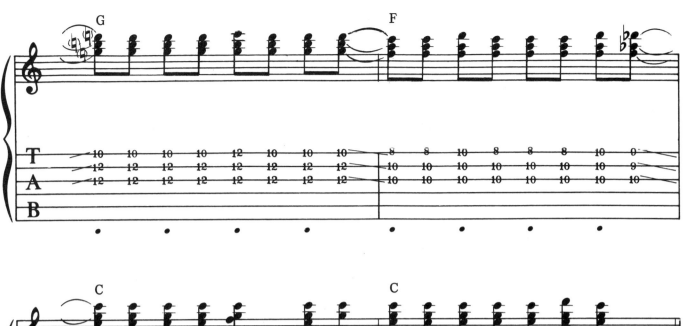

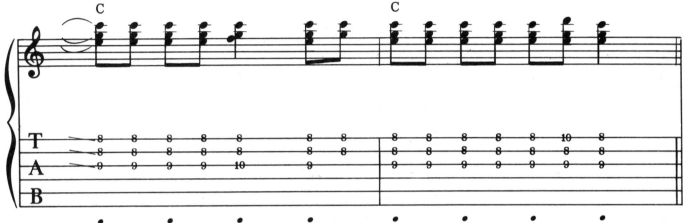

## Notes On "Ready Teddy"

♩ = 200. This is a fast song, and though the vocal part involves a swing, the guitar break is played straight.

Doublestops are used for most of the break, with partial chords for the last few bars. The slides are longer than usual — they begin on the halfbeat. Add your little finger for the high G note in bars 4 & 8 and for the high F in bars 6 & 10. Add your 3rd finger for the F note in bars 13 - 16.

Use these chord shapes for the last four bars:

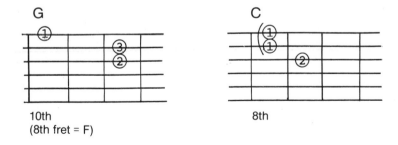

Add your little finger on the top string when holding the G chord. Add your 3rd finger on the 3rd string then little finger on the top string when holding the C chord.

# RIP IT UP

Words and Music by ROBERT A BLACKWELL and JOHN MARASCALCO

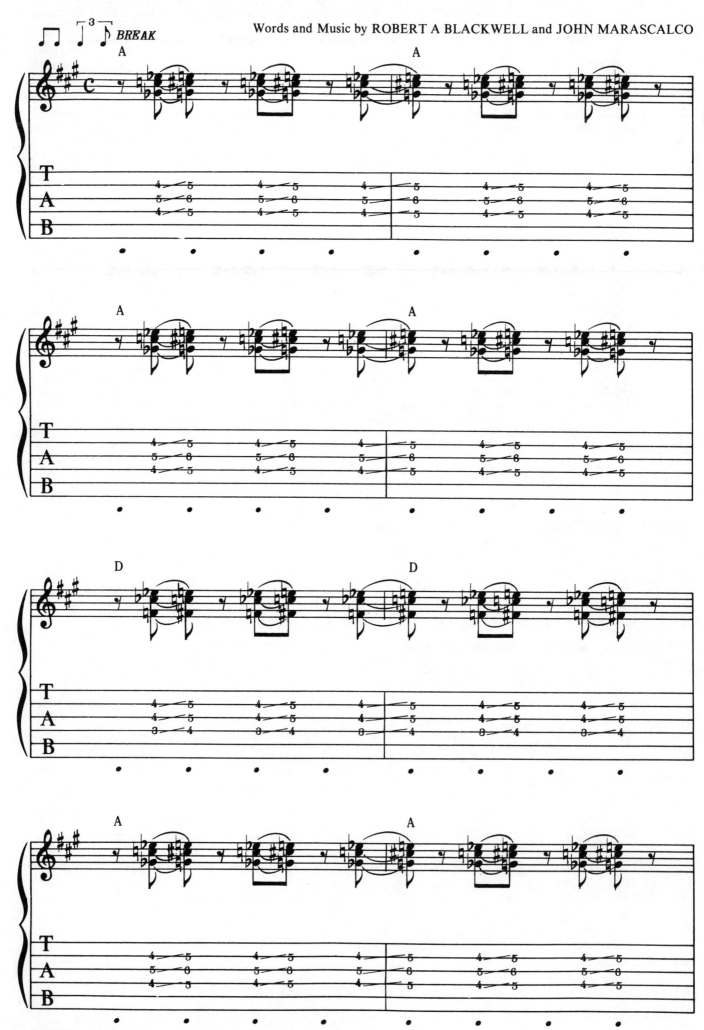

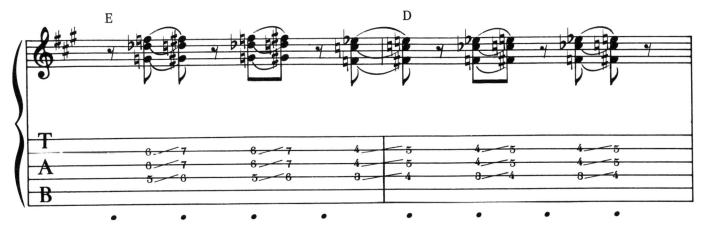

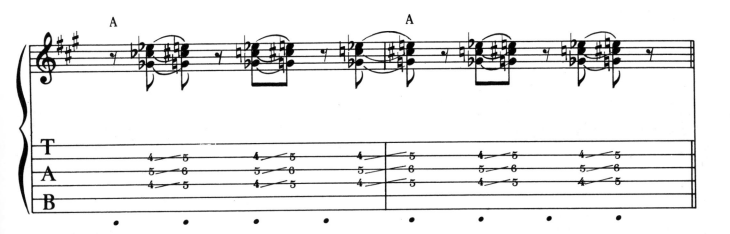

## Notes On "Rip It Up"

♩ = 200. This song is fast, with a jumpy, rhythmic guitar break.

Hold these shapes for this break (slide them from one fret below):

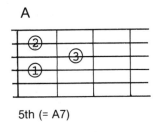

5th (= A7)

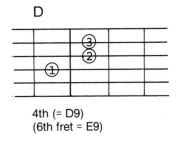

4th (= D9)
(6th fret = E9)

Scotty probably holds these fuller chord shapes:

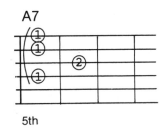

5th

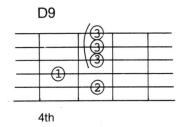

4th

The note C♭ is played like a B. The rests after the strums indicated in the standard notation mean you should stop or damp the strings — release the finger pressure on the strings, as explained on page 7.

Don't forget to swing the rhythm.

# SHAKE RATTLE & ROLL

Words and Music by CHARLES E CALHOUN

## Notes On "Shake Rattle And Roll"

♩ = 200. This is another fast song in cut time, and like the last has a swing rhythm.

The break starts with two pull-offs one after the other — use your 1st & 2nd fingers. The alternating thumb style is used from bar 4 — see page 7. Use these shapes:

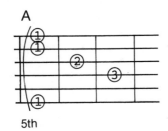

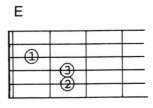

Add your little finger for the 6th & 7th notes. The little finger slides from the 3rd fret to the 2nd fret, 2nd string in the last two bars while you're holding the E chord. The run in the B bar is a popular one — use your 1st finger for the starting B note and 3rd for the C♯. Then move your 3rd up for the D♯. Use your 2nd finger for the high D♯ at the end of the B bar, which allows your 1st finger to fret the 2nd string F♯ note more easily.

# THAT'S ALL RIGHT

Words and Music by ARTHUR CAUDUP

## Notes On "That's All Right"

♩ = 204. Another fast song, this time *without* a swing.

Use your 2nd & 3rd fingers for the first two doublestops, and then bar with your 1st finger at the 2nd fret. Slide up the doublestop in bars 3 & 5, then quickly off from any lower fret. The run of bass notes can be damped slightly, as are the bass notes in the alternating thumb style from bar 10 — see page 7.

You can use your 1st & 2nd fingers on the 2nd string to help the 3rd finger bend the string in bar 8.

Here are the shapes you can use for the alternating thumb bars:

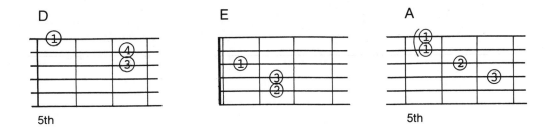

Add your little finger for the G natural note on the top string when holding the E position. Add your little finger for the 6th note on the 2nd string when holding the A position.

# TOO MUCH

Words and Music by LEE ROSENBERG and BERNARD WEINMAN

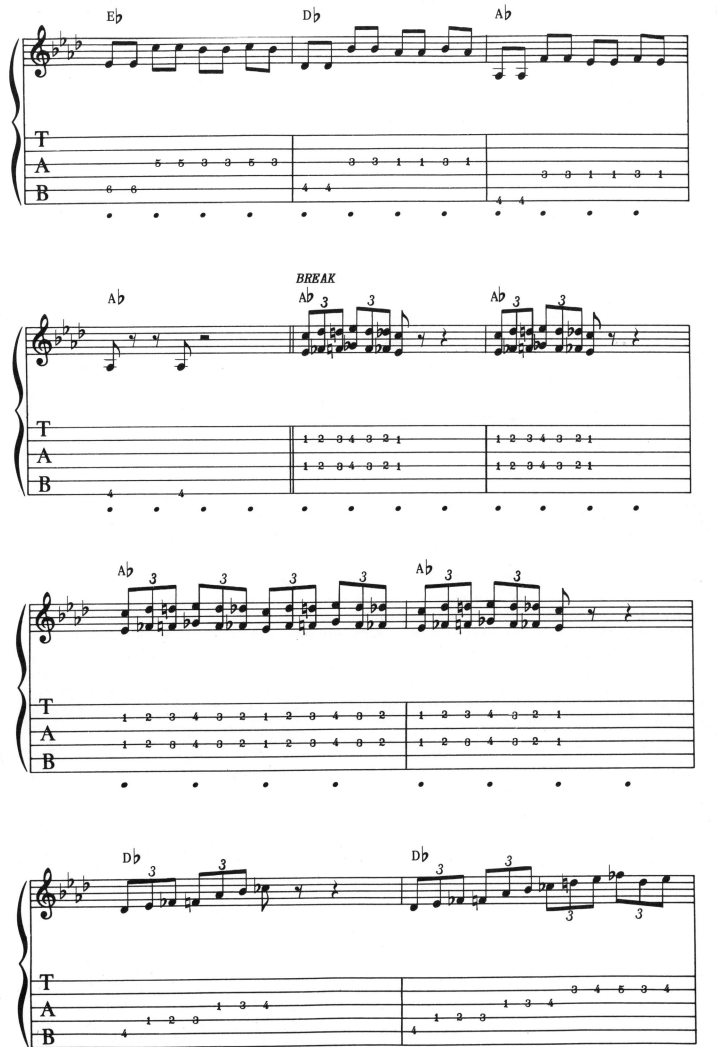

### Notes On "Too Much"

♩ = 116. This song has a slow to moderate tempo — and a swing rhythm.

Take all the notes down one fret to the key of D if you prefer to work in a familiar key. Use your little finger then 3rd and 1st fingers for the introduction and vocal backing. Stop the last two A♭ notes short. For the chromatic run at the start of the break, you can use your 1st & 2nd or 2nd & 3rd fingers (or even a bar with your 1st finger).

Hold your left hand in the 1st position for the run in bar 5 of the break. Switch to the 3rd position on the D natural note halfway through bar 6. Then switch to the 4th position in bar 8 by using the 3rd finger for the D♭ note. Then stay in the 4th position to the end — moving the 1st finger back one fret and sliding forward on two occasions.

Use your thumb and 2nd finger for the doublestop runs and down/up/down strokes for the triplet runs.

# TUTTI FRUTTI

Words and Music by R PENNIMAN and D LA BOSTRIE

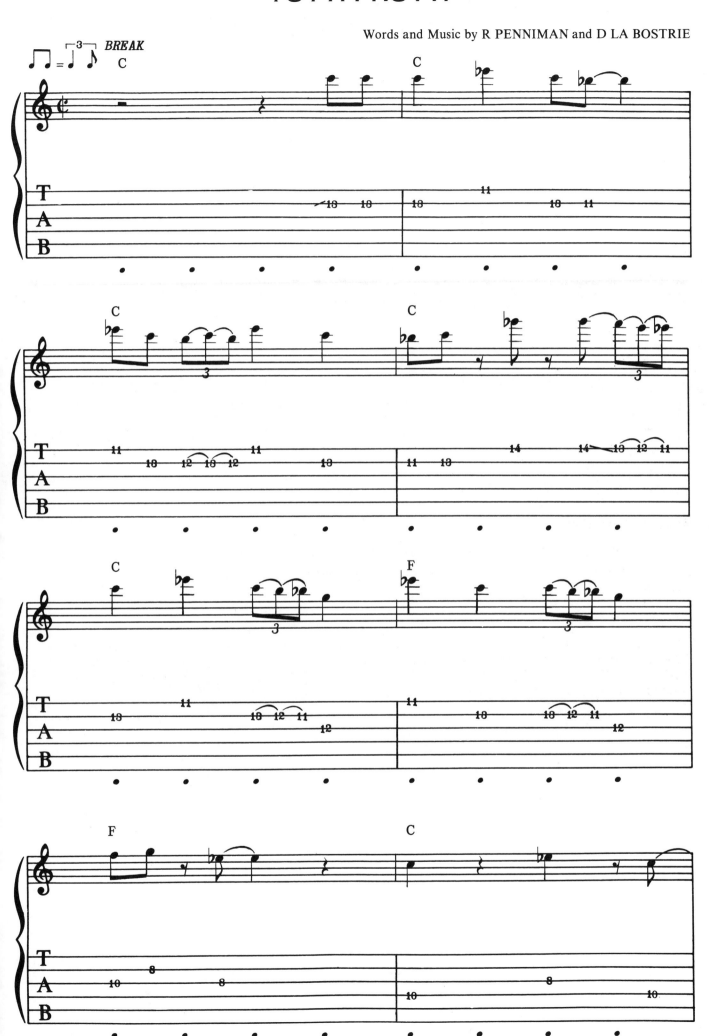

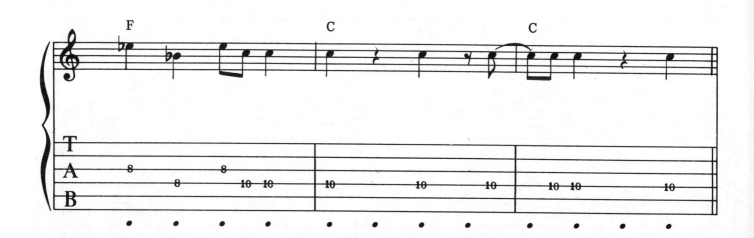

**Notes On "Tutti Frutti"**

♩ = 224. The swing rhythm is not too noticeable at this fast speed, but it's still there!

Start in the 11th position with your left hand, then switch to the 8th position in bar 7. Stop some of the notes as indicated in the standard music notation.

# YOU'RE A HEARTBREAKER

Words and Music by JACK SALLEE

*INTRODUCTION*

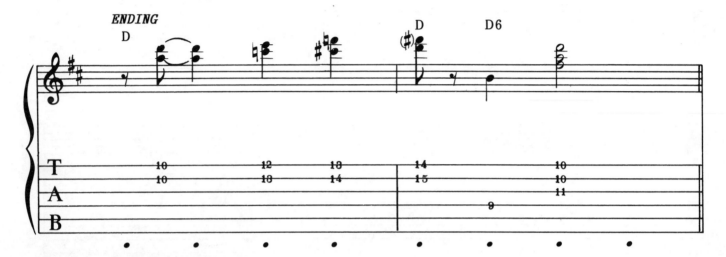

## Notes On "You're A Heartbreaker"

♩ = 200. This is another fast cut-time song. Only occasional notes are swung slightly during the break.

Scotty uses these shapes to introduce the song:

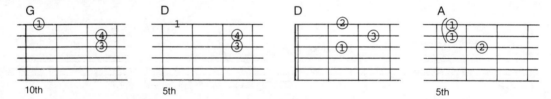

The bass notes are damped slightly — see page 7.

Start the first tag with these three shapes:

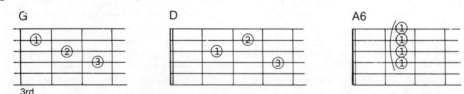

Bar across the top four strings at the 7th fret for the run in the last two bars of the first tag. Stretch the 4th finger to the 11th fret of the 2nd string!

Use your 1st & 2nd fingers for the start of the second tag, and add your 4th finger. The 6th notes in bar 3 are fretted by your 1st & 2nd fingers, then move to your 2nd & 3rd fingers, then finally back to 1st & 2nd. The last three notes are harmonics — press lightly *directly* over the 7th fret wire, strike the string with your right hand and take off your left hand finger quickly.

The D6 at the end of the song is fingered like this:

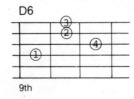

The root note is on the top string with this position.

Printed by Loader Jackson Printers Arlesey Beds 3/90